W9-BVS-018

RICHARD SCARRY'S
Great Big Schoolhouse
Readers

Hop, Hop, and Away!

Illustrated by Huck Scarry
Written by Erica Farber

New York / London
www.sterlingpublishing.com/kids

Today is show-and-tell.

Huckle packed his backpack.

Huckle packed his lunch.

Huckle packed his pet frog.

Hop, hop, and away!

Huckle's frog hopped away.

Lowly got the frog.

Phew!

Good job, Lowly!

Huckle went to school.

Hop, hop, and away!

Huckle's frog hopped away.

Skip got the frog.

Thank you, Skip!

It was time for show-and-tell.

Arthur showed
his ant farm.

Ella showed her fancy doll.

Bridget had a whistle.

Bridget blew it.

Hop, hop, and away!

Huckle's frog hopped away.

It hopped on Ella. Oh, no!

Huckle got his frog.
It was not his turn.

Lowly was next.
He told a joke.

Molly showed a book.
Skip had a big ball.
He bounced the ball.

Bam! Bam!

Frances had a volcano.
She put stuff into it.

At last it was Huckle's turn.

He showed his frog.

BOOM! went the volcano.

BOOM! BOOM!

Lava went up in the air.

Lava went all over.

Bridget blew
her whistle.

Hop, hop, and away!
Huckle's frog hopped away.
It hopped on Skip.

Bam went Skip's ball.

The ball hit Molly's book.

The book hit the ant farm.

BOOM! CRASH!

Hop, hop, and away!
Huckle's frog hopped
on Miss Honey.

She smiled.

Show & Tel